Pups Stick Together!

A GOLDEN BOOK • NEW YORK

ISBN 978-1-5247-6877-5

rhcbooks.com

MANUFACTURED IN CHINA

"Calling all pups!" says Ryder.

Chase

Marshall

Marshall

Skye

Rubble

Rocky

Zuma

Everest

Tracker

Can you track down the picture that is different?

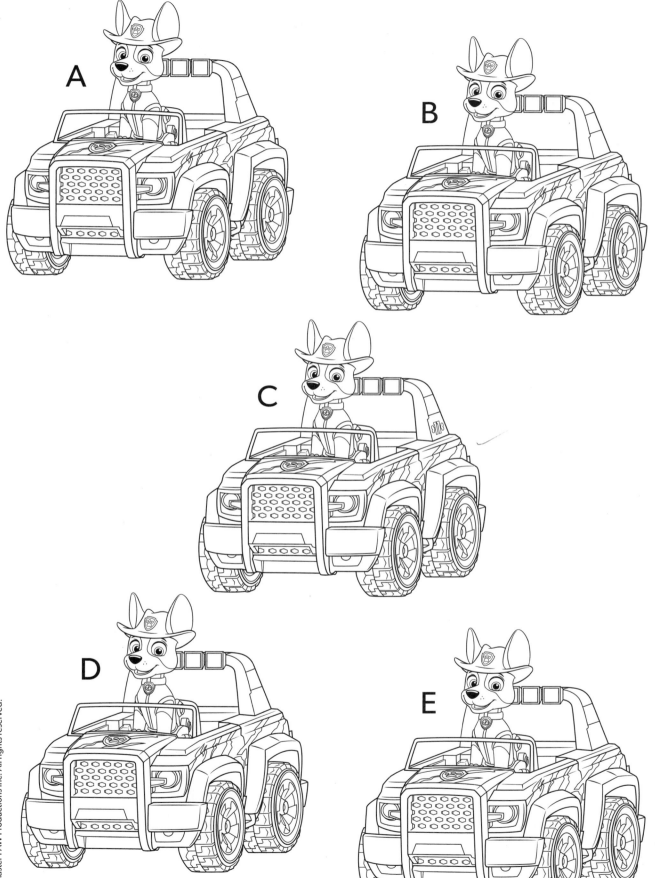

A

B

C

D

E

ANSWER: C.

Match each driver to his or her vehicle.

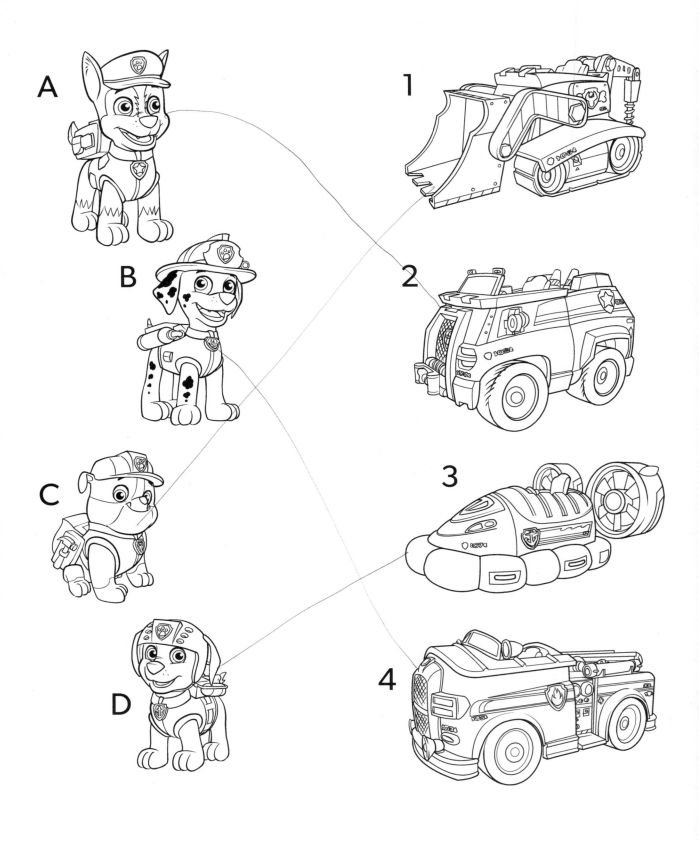

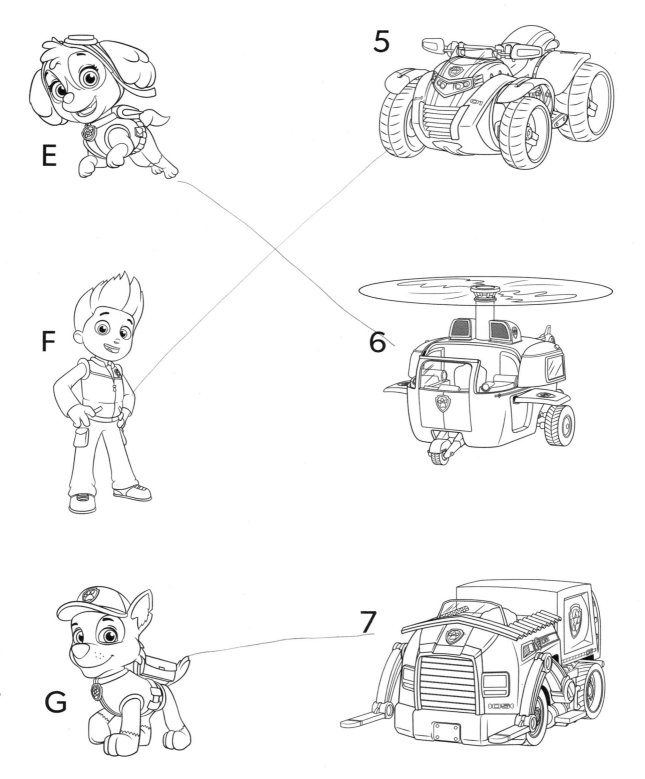

E

F

G

5

6

7

Help Marshall find the path to his fire truck.

START

FINISH

ANSWER:

Ready for a ruff-ruff rescue!

Find the picture of Marshall that is different.

Marshall is one *pawsome* fire pup,
but sometimes he can be a little clumsy.

Or a lot clumsy.

"Here I come, Cali," calls Marshall.
"Ladder up, and— Whoa!"

"I'm okay," says Marshall.

"Today Marshall will attempt the fastest fire-rescue course run ever!" announces Mayor Goodway.

Ready! Set! Go!

Marshall almost trips on the tires.

"He's making really good time," says Ryder.
"Go, Marshall!"

Marshall shoots water from his
water cannons and hits the target.

Oh, no! There's a real fire!
Marshall stops to put it out.

"Now I just have to get to the
finish line," says Marshall.

"Uh-oh. Marshall didn't get
the record," Ryder says.

"That's okay," Marshall says.
"I did my best."

"You stopped to put out a real fire. That makes you a real Adventure Bay hero," the mayor says.

Three barks for Marshall!

Back at the Lookout,
Ryder gets a message from Katie.

A train Katie is on has been stopped by a rockslide!
The PAW Patrol is called to help.

Rocky and Rubble come running!

The PAW Patrol reporting for duty!

Ryder tells the team about Katie's train.

Ryder needs Rubble to lift the rocks off the tracks.

And Rocky needs to fix the tracks!

Rubble on the double!

Green means go!

Ryder leads the way!

The rocks have stopped the train on an old bridge!

Katie looks out the train window.
"The PAW Patrol is here!"

"The tracks are okay," Ryder says. "We just need to clear away the rocks."

Rubble gets to work moving the rocks.

At the bottom of the bridge, Ryder finds a broken beam!

Rocky can fix the beam with a log, but he can't get the log to the bottom of the steep hill.

Ryder calls for Chase because his truck has a winch.

Chase hooks his winch to the log. But who can move the log over the edge of the hill?

Rubble can do it!

The rocks have been cleared away, and the track is fixed.
The train is ready to roll!

"Thank you, PAW Patrol!"

Rubble, Rocky, and Chase are all good pups!

When the job is done, it's time for fun!

Rubble is on a roll!

Draw a basketball for the pups to play with.

Draw a basketball for the pups to play with.

Marshall shows off with a Dalmatian dunk!

Here comes Rocky's spin-and-shoot!

Oh, no! Chase hurt his paw.

If there's a medical emergency, just yelp for help!

Marshall takes an X-ray.
"It's just a sprain," he says.

"You'll be okay," Marshall says
after he bandages Chase's paw.

"Great work, Marshall," says Ryder.

Hooray for the PAW Patrol!